MANGO THE MANATEE

Story by: Lindsey Michele Clark
Illustrated by: Leah Lopez

A Message from the Author

This book is dedicated to all the amazing children in my life that have contributed to making "Auntie life" such a wonderful one. I thank God for all of them and also for creating these beautiful manatees, along with giving me such a passion for both. Above all, I thank God for blessing me with such a supportive and incredible husband through all my adventures. I am a better woman because of you.

–Lindsey

https://www.facebook.com/mangothemanatee/

About the Illustrator

Leah Lopez is an award-winning artist and cartoonist. Leah began drawing at the age of 2, and she eventually adopted her favorite medium- colored pencils. At age 16, Leah started teaching children how to draw and color cartoons through a business she founded- Leah's Cartooning Parties, Inc. Recently, Leah has discovered a passion of bring stories to life through illustrating.

Instagram: @leah_lopez_artwork

ISBN 978-0-692-88239-9
All Rights Reserved
Copyright 2017
Published by IngramSpark

Mango the manatee was eating a delicious lunch
of seagrass and hyacinths with her mother,
when she felt a cold rush of water against her thick gray skin.

"Brrrrr!" Mango yelped with a shiver, "that was chilly!"
"Yes it was," replied Mango's mother.
"The ocean tide is bringing in colder water since it's almost winter,
which means it's time for us to move to a warmer place.
We can't stay here once it gets much colder or we will get very sick."

Mango had not yet left the ocean's coastline since she was so young,
and had no idea where this warmer water was.
She was excited to explore and make new friends.
"Where will we go and what is it like?" Mango asked.
"It's a beautiful place called the Crystal River where springs of warm water
bubble up from the ground through the sand
and keep the water warm and sparkling clear,"
Mango's mother answered.

"Wow! That sounds like magic!" Mango squealed.
"There will also be many other manatees
and some will look different than us without any barnacles on their backs,"
Mango's mother told her.

"No barnacles?" Mango was surprised.
She loved her barnacles. They were her own special jewelry
and her mother always told her how beautiful they were.
She had never seen a manatee without them.
"How sad they don't have any barnacle jewelry."

Mango's mother laughed,
"Oh Mango, yes your barnacle jewelry is beautiful,
but those without them are just as beautiful! We have barnacles
only because we live most of the year by the ocean's coast.
Barnacles can't grow in fresh water rivers
and if we stay there long enough even ours will fall off."

"WHAT?!?" Mango was shocked.
"I had no idea my barnacles could fall off!"

"Yes, and they might! Now come on,
let's get going so you can meet those new friends!"
Mango's mother called as she began to swim away.

On their journey to the Crystal River
they encountered many wonderful treasures and creatures.
They passed dolphins.
"Hello dolphins!" Mango waved, "You look very lovely and graceful today!"

They saw sea turtles.
"Hi sea turtles!" Mango shouted, "I love your pretty turtle shells!"

They swam along side small silvery mullet fish.
"Hello fish!" Mango cheered, "You're doing a great job swimming!"

They also passed many boats. "Hi boats!" Mango called,
"Thank you for going slow so we can swim around you and not bonk
our heads or backs when we come up for a breath of air!"

Finally they made it into a long stretch of crystal clear water. Mango saw many other manatees with smooth beautiful gray skin without barnacles.

"I'm going to go introduce myself to some new friends!"
Mango called to her mother as she flipped her tail
and sailed through the water.
She couldn't wait to go play with all the new manatees.

"Hi, I'm Mango!" she said to a particularly pretty manatee
that she just knew would be her friend.
"Can I play with you guys?"

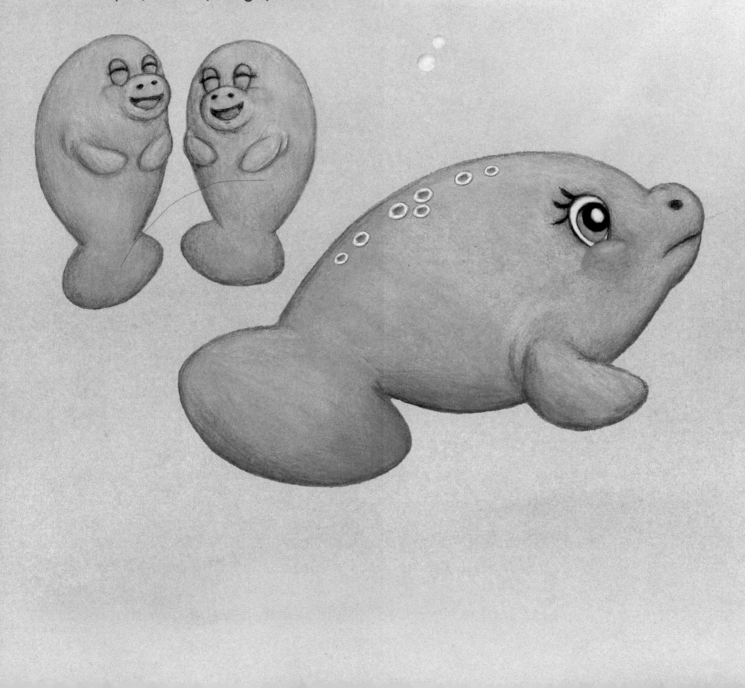

"Mango! What kind of name is Mango!?
That's a fruit and not a name for a manatee!"
The manatee laughed, "I'm Betsy, and that's a real manatee name.
Not like Mango – Tango – Banana Fana – Fango!" Betsy sang out
and all the other manatees around her
broke out into loud peals of laughter.

"Why do you have those weird spots on your back and look so different from all of us?" Another manatee asked. "They're my barnacle jewelry," Mango whispered.

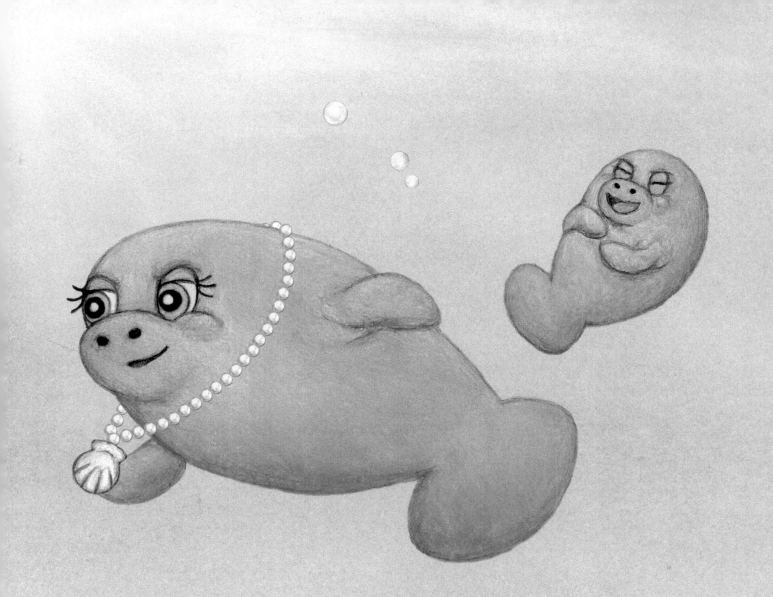

"AHH HAA HAAA HA!" The other manatees laughed even harder.
"That's not jewelry!" Betsy snickered, "this is real jewelry!"
She showed off a beautiful shell tied around her neck
before she and the other manatees all swam away
and left Mango by herself.

Mango was heartbroken, and sped off as fast as she could swim
to find her mother as she wiped the tears off her face.
"Mom!" She cried as she rounded a corner and saw
her mother's familiar face and barnacles,
"The manatees here are MEAN!
They made fun of my name and my barnacle jewelry.
They're terrible! I want to go back to the ocean!"

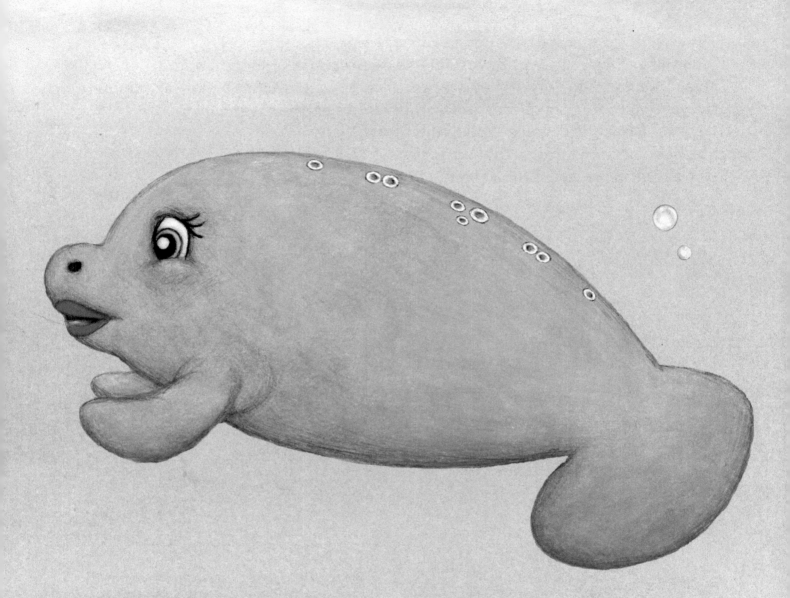

"Oh Mango, I'm so sorry but we can't go back."
Mango's mother held her while Mango sobbed in her arms.
"Sometimes new adventures are tough, and friends can be difficult,
but you were made perfectly with your ocean barnacles
and are beautiful inside and out."

"They were so mean and laughed at me!
I don't like them and will never talk to them again!" Mango pouted.
"Sweet Mango, I'm sorry they weren't nice to you." Mango's mother hugged her.
"Do you want to go explore some other areas of the river?
There is a beautiful place called the Three Sisters
that has those magical bubbling springs I told you about.
That might make you feel better."

Mango was still upset but reluctantly agreed,
and began to slowly swim towards the mysterious bubbling springs.
She had to swim a little harder around the bend
because the flow of water had gotten much stronger.
She was very used to the change of tides and currents in the
ocean and enjoyed the familiar reminder of home.

The closer to the springs she got, the warmer the water was.
It felt like a soft cozy blanket had wrapped her up in a hug
and it made her smile.
Mango couldn't believe how sparkly and clear the water was too.
She couldn't wait to get to the Three Sisters
and see just how magical this place was.

As she came around the corner
to the beautiful bubbling water
she saw that the mean manatee, Betsy,
was sunbathing alone next to the magnificent springs.
"Ugh!" She sulked and was about to turn around
to swim away as fast as she could
when she saw Betsy start to flop back and forth.

"Help! Help!" Cried Betsy, "I'm stuck on a fishing line!"
Mango thought about whether to swim away
and just leave her behind. After all,
Betsy had been very mean to her.
But what would she want to happen
if she was the one stuck she asked herself?
Mango knew what she would want done for herself,
and that to leave Betsy alone and swim away
wouldn't be the right thing to do.

She slowly turned back around and swam towards Betsy
bracing for her to say mean things to her.
Instead Betsy just watched her silently with wide eyes.
Mango carefully and nervously unwrapped the line from Betsy's tail.
She half expected Betsy to make fun of her for doing it wrong
when instead...

Betsy launched herself onto Mango giving her a great big hug.
"Thank you so much for saving me!" Gulped Betsy.
"I'm so sorry I was mean to you earlier.
I shouldn't have said those mean things.
I thought your barnacle jewelry was beautiful
and I was jealous so I lashed out. I'm so sorry."
"Oh!" Exclaimed Mango in surprise,
"You're very welcome."

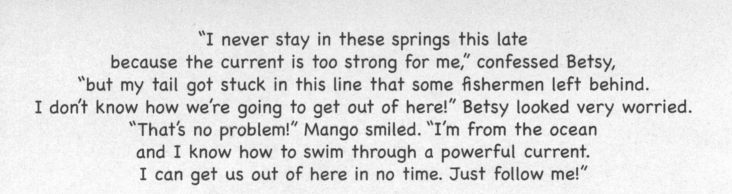

"I never stay in these springs this late
because the current is too strong for me," confessed Betsy,
"but my tail got stuck in this line that some fishermen left behind.
I don't know how we're going to get out of here!" Betsy looked very worried.
"That's no problem!" Mango smiled. "I'm from the ocean
and I know how to swim through a powerful current.
I can get us out of here in no time. Just follow me!"

Mango led Betsy through the tough water passageway
and back into the safety of the river. They arrived out of breath,
but safe and sound. "Thank you so much!" Betsy exhaled,
"You really saved me and you didn't have to. You are the best manatee ever."
"It was how I would want to be treated,"
Mango answered with a smile.

"Well, I didn't act how I should have earlier
and I'm so sorry," Betsy apologized again.
"Here, please take my shell necklace. You deserve it
and I want you to have it. Tomorrow will you come play with us?
I'd love to introduce you to all my friends!"
"Wow, thanks!" Mango squeaked. "Yes, I would love to!"

Mango couldn't wipe the huge grin off her face
and was so happy she did the right thing.
She couldn't wait to swim home and tell her mother
all about her new friend and her beautiful new jewelry.